Cyr...
Charlie's... ...ght Out

Shoo Rayner

PUFFIN BOOKS

Published by the Penguin Group
Penguin Books Ltd, 27 Wrights Lane, London W8 5TZ, England
Penguin Putnam Inc., 375 Hudson Street, New York, New York 10014, USA
Penguin Books Australia Ltd, Ringwood, Victoria, Australia
Penguin Books Canada Ltd, 10 Alcorn Avenue, Toronto, Ontario, Canada M4V 3B2
Penguin Books (NZ) Ltd, 182–190 Wairau Road, Auckland 10, New Zealand

Penguin Books Ltd, Registered Offices: Harmondsworth, Middlesex, England

Published in Puffin Books 1993
10 9 8 7

Text and illustrations copyright © Shoo Rayner, 1993
All rights reserved

The moral right of the author/illustrator has been asserted

Filmset in Monotype Bembo Schoolbook

Reproduction by Anglia Graphics Ltd, Bedford

Made and printed in Great Britain by Clays Ltd, St Ives plc

Except in the United States of America, this book is sold subject to the condition
that it shall not, by way of trade or otherwise, be lent, re-sold, hired out, or otherwise
circulated without the publisher's prior consent in any form of binding or cover other
than that in which it is published and without a similar condition including this
condition being imposed on the subsequent purchaser

691617
MORAY COUNCIL
Department of Technical
& Leisure Services
JB

Contents

THE INCREDIBLY HOT DAY

Cyril's cat, Charlie, woke up
feeling hot and scratchy. He drank
some water from his bowl, then he
poked his head out of the cat-flap.
The sun was shining brightly in a
clear blue sky.

It's going to be an incredibly hot
day, he thought. It was already
quite hot.

When Cyril came into the garden it was so hot that he was wearing shorts. "Looks like a good day for gardening," he said to himself.

Cyril's shed was very old and very small.

It was so small that he had to take the wheelbarrow out before he could get to his mower.

Charlie sat in the shade under the wheelbarrow. He watched Cyril go up and down, up and down, up and down as he pushed the lawn-mower along.

He was just about falling asleep
when Cyril wheeled the barrow
away and started to fill it up with
grass cuttings.

Humph! thought Charlie, if I sleep in this hot sun I'll get sunstroke. His paws felt hot on the concrete path as he tripped to the bottom of the garden. There he found a cool, shady place under the old lilac tree.

There he lay, fast asleep until
Cyril dumped all his grass cuttings
on top of him!

Humph! thought Charlie, if he's
going to be gardening all day
then I'll go and sleep under the
car. That will be safe.

By now it was getting *very* hot, even under the car. Charlie could hear Cyril whistling in the garden shed. Charlie was soon fast asleep, dreaming of cool saucers of milk laid out on a cold dairy floor.

RRRRM! RRRRRM! RRRRRM!

went the car.

MMMRRRRREEEEEOW! went
Charlie, as he ran for his life!
Half-way up a cherry tree he
stopped for breath and saw Cyril
driving off down the road.

Charlie came down the tree and walked into the garden. He was looking for a safe, cool, shady place where he could sleep for the rest of the day. But something odd had been going on. Cyril's tools were laid out on the path.

The grass had been cleared away around the shed. He noticed that there was a Charlie-sized gap under the shed. Perhaps he could just squeeze through.

It was lovely and cool under there.
He stretched out in the dry dust
and was soon fast asleep again.

He didn't hear Cyril come home. He didn't hear him walking up and down the path as he drank a mug of tea. He might have heard Cyril say, "Right! Here we go then." But he did hear the first crash as Cyril's axe hit the side of the old shed!

23

Charlie was terrified and tried to squeeze and squash himself out from under the shed. Cyril didn't see him and carried on banging and bashing away like a madman.

It's the sun, thought Charlie, it's
gone to his head. Then, suddenly,
he popped out and landed in a
flower-bed just as the shed
collapsed in on itself.

Cyril cleared away the rotten old
wood, then he unloaded some
large wooden panels off the roof
of the car.

He hammered some nails

and screwed some screws

and soon there was a brand new shed standing where the old one had been.

While Cyril put all his tools into
the new shed, Charlie decided to
investigate.

He had a good sniff round. He
leaned against it for a little while.
He sharpened his claws on it.
When he decided it was all right
he crawled underneath it.

I think I'll be safe under here, he thought to himself. Then, with a large, sleepy smile on his face, Charlie settled down for the rest of the day. Cyril whistled quietly to himself and finished off sorting out his nice new shed.

CHARLIE'S NIGHT OUT

Cyril was going away. He was going to stay with his daughter and look after his two grandchildren for the night.

He hustled and bustled around the house, packing and tidying. Charlie thought that it was safer to go outside. He found a quiet spot to catch up on some sleep.

When he heard Cyril's daughter arrive with her children he went round to the front of the house. Kate and Sally loved Charlie. They didn't have a cat of their own. So when they came to see Grandpa they always made a fuss of Charlie.

Charlie didn't mind at all. He let
them hug him and stroke him and
tickle him under the chin.

When it was time to go Cyril took Charlie into the kitchen and showed him his special bowl that had a clock on it. When it was time for supper the lid would pop up.

"Here you are, Charlie," said
Cyril, "there's lots of water for
you and your supper will be ready
at the normal time. I'll only be
gone one night, so you won't get
lonely."

Charlie was quite used to Cyril going away so he purred to let him know that he would be all right. Then he sat on the front wall and watched as they drove off down the street.

They hadn't been gone very long when a post van pulled up outside the house. The usual postman was a friend of Charlie's who always said hello. This was not the usual postman. This postman had a large parcel. He went to the front door and rang the bell. Of course nobody answered, so he went round to the back door.

Charlie followed him and tried to make friends, but this postman didn't seem to like cats. Charlie thought he smelled of dogs. The postman knocked on the door a few times but still nobody answered. He muttered to himself, wrote something down in a book and put the parcel on the doorstep, then he went to his van and drove away.

Well! thought Charlie, he wasn't very friendly. Then he settled down in one of his favourite sunny spots and dreamed the afternoon away.

A huge crack of thunder woke him. He closed his eyes and ran for the cat-flap. Kerbang! Something hit him on the head. He opened his eyes to see what it was. There, where the cat-flap should have been, was the parcel. The postman had blocked the cat-flap!

By now great, big, wet blobs of rain were falling. Charlie was getting very wet. He tried to move the parcel away but it was too heavy for him. He ran across the lawn and squeezed under the shed. There was nothing for it but to sit and wait until Cyril came home the next day.

It was a long, cold night. Cyril came back the next day, but there was no Charlie to greet him. Cyril went through all the rooms in the house but Charlie was nowhere to be found. In the kitchen the lid had popped up on Charlie's bowl but nothing had been eaten.

Cyril began to worry. He opened
the back door and saw the parcel.
Then he knew what had
happened.

Charlie heard Cyril calling him. He crawled out from under the shed. He stood on the path shivering. His fur was all damp and matted and he looked very sorry for himself.

Cyril took him into the kitchen and rubbed him dry with a big, soft towel. He gave him some fresh food and some cream from the milk.

"Now let's see what's in this parcel," said Cyril, as he cut through the packaging. When it was undone there was a lot of cardboard and something that looked a bit like an igloo.

When Charlie finished his food
Cyril picked him up and put him
inside it. "It's for you," he said.

It was lovely and warm, just the sort of place to have a really good sleep. "It's a cat bed," said Cyril. "Cats are supposed to really like them."

Charlie loved it. He licked himself clean and settled down. Soon Cyril could hear a loud purring and knew that Charlie was all right.

"It's a funny old world," he chuckled, "the one thing that could keep you warm and dry was the thing that kept you out in the rain!" Then he went off to unpack and left Charlie to have a really good sleep.